# JUN(
## FOR ⌐..⌐⌐DREN

**Kenneth Anderson** (1910–1974) was a hunter, nature enthusiast and chronicler of wildlife. His hunting expeditions involved several close encounters with man-eating tigers, rogue elephants, leopards and other wild animals. He wrote about eight books and sixty short stories which recount many of his real-life adventures and hunting exploits in the jungles of South India. In 2000, his collected works, *The Kenneth Anderson Omnibus*, were published in two volumes.

He spent most of his life in Bangalore, where he was employed with an aeronautics company. Anderson's invaluable contribution to shikar literature in India continues to inspire scores of wildlife lovers.

Visit www.facebook.com/groups/ kennethanderson to know more about the author.

# JUNGLE TALES
# FOR CHILDREN

### Kenneth Anderson

RUPA

First published in 2012 by
**Rupa Publications India Pvt. Ltd.**
7/16, Ansari Road, Daryaganj
New Delhi 110 002

*Sales Centres:*

Allahabad Bengaluru Chennai
Hyderabad Jaipur Kathmandu
Kolkata Mumbai

10 9 8 7 6 5 4 3 2 1

Printed in India by
Replika Press Pvt Ltd
310-311 EPIP Kundli
Haryana 131028 India

# Contents

# Foreword

My boyhood in India was an exquisite blend of contradictions. Schoolmates from several religious faiths, languages, ethnic backgrounds, socio-economic groups and cultures played together happily, enjoying each other's festivals and food, revelling in their differences.

If my new home, Australia, can be described as a 'melting pot' of cultures, then my native land of India is best described as a 'thali'.

A large plate, served with a vast variety of delicious, different foods, different colours, textures, flavours, spices and temperatures— never to be mixed but savoured slowly and individually as part of a complete, satisfying and fulfilling feast.

In those early years after the British departed, we were left with adults who loved hunting wild animals for sport and children who loved the joyful books about animals showing human characteristics in their daily lives. Anthropomorphism is a phenomenon that goes back to the Palaeolithic times.

At school we were enchanted by *Grimms' Fairy Tales* by the Brothers Grimm, *Alice's Adventures in Wonderland* by Lewis Carroll and *The Jungle Book* by Rudyard Kipling. We then graduated to *The Tale of Peter Rabbit* by Beatrix Potter, *The Wind in the Willows* by Kenneth Grahame, *The Lion, the Witch and the Wardrobe* by C. S. Lewis and *Winnie-the-Pooh* by A. A. Milne.

Sadly, these charming books are no longer read widely. Instead, we have violent video games which occupy the fingers but not the brains of our children. Bringing horror into their homes and cruelty into their hearts.

The most beautiful word ever written, in any language, at any time, in any country, in human history, came from India. From the Upanishads 8,000 years ago. 'Ahimsa'—non-violence to any living being.

Mahatma Gandhi bravely told the truth: 'A nation is judged by the way she treats her animals.' On this basis, all nations must be judged with unsparing harshness.

In law school we are constantly told of our 'Duty of Care'. But how often are we told that we have a 'Duty to Care'? Well, there is one place. In the Indian Constitution (Article 51A [g]). 'It shall be the fundamental duty of every citizen of India to protect and improve the Natural Environment, including forests, lakes, rivers and wildlife, and to have compassion for all living creatures.'

But as Hamlet ruefully observed, '...it is a custom, more honour'd in the breach than the observance.'

Gandhi would recoil in horror to know that every week 3 billion animals are now tortured and killed for food, fashion, fad or fun...or in useless laboratory experiments... Every week!

These are crimes of unimaginable proportions. Crimes against so-called 'farm' animals are so egregious that, if committed against a domestic pet, or an 'iconic' animal like a tiger, they would land the miscreant in prison. But these crimes go unpunished. So the cruellest mammalian primate, with an opposable thumb, an insatiable appetite and arrogance beyond compare, is responsible for the greatest ecocide in human history.

As a boy, and then as a young man, I held Kenneth Anderson in awe. To this day, I don't

X

know why my family cheerfully addressed him as 'Jock'. I was spellbound by his prodigious knowledge of the jungles, rivers, creeks and tanks; the animals, birds and insects—and his fascination with snakes; his deep affection for the hospitable, gentle people who lived in the jungle; his eccentric nature and desire to spend as much of his waking hours as possible in the jungle, as far away from human interference as possible. An hour spent away from the jungle was, to Jock, a wasted hour.

He was often alone. But he was never lonely. Like all strong men, he stood strongest when he was alone. I felt singularly honoured when his son, Donald, wrote: 'I wish you could have spent more time with my father. He would have been proud to see the man you have become.'

I have read every book ever written by Jock Anderson. And, through the generosity of Donald, they occupy pride of place in my library. They are constant reminders of another time—more innocent perhaps, when the world was a simpler place. When we still had a chance to see the future and do something to protect it. Alas, with each passing day, we see it disappearing before our eyes. Newer generations know less, care less and want more. The beauty of the Indian jungle and the wild animals that live there are tragically under threat from human encroachment as never before.

I am delighted that there are so many remarkable young people who have discovered Jock Anderson, his writing and his son, Donald. Their stories are all interwoven into the rich tapestry through which the fascinating history of India is revealed. I had the unbridled joy of meeting several of these young people, and I am astonished to see the reverence they have for a man they know only through his books and their jungle travels with his beloved son.

I hope this book is read by every Indian child. I read it again today and it took my mind's eye back to another time. Another India. Half a century ago. When the Indian jungle was teeming with animals from species too diverse to count. When the rivers were clean. When birdsong could be heard above the sounds of the river and the wind in the trees. When a young boy sat alone, daydreaming, amongst the watermelons, on the banks of the Cauvery and Arkavarthi rivers at Sangam. Experiencing the solitary joy only an innocent heart could understand—and only Jock Anderson could describe.

I am eternally grateful for the man. His memories. And his books.

Philip Malcolm Wollen
Australia

# A Word to Parents
# Who Buy This Book

In writing this book for children, I have tried
to keep three purposes in view.

The first has been to relate something new
and unusual, slightly different from the kind
of stories to which they have so long been
accustomed; and at the same time, something
that would hold their interest in each story.

My second purpose has been to teach them a little about a few of the wild animals and birds that exist along with us in this beautiful land in which we live. In doing this, I want to educate them to some small extent in what may loosely be called Natural History, while arousing in the minds of the youngsters a love of Nature and an affection and gentleness for the dumb creatures that live around us. For they do really need this kindness in a world of increasing cruelty and harshness on the part of men towards the humble beasts of the forest, as well as those that serve us in civilization.

Lastly, into each story I have tried to weave a moral or lesson, sometimes several of them, that impinge and impress themselves on the minds of the boy or girl who reads them. This, really, is my main purpose. I am convinced that many of us would have been far better men and women today had we been taught better when we were young. Some of us were taught by the cane and threats of severe punishment;

XVI

perhaps a few of us were not taught at all. In both cases, the results may not have been very good. The method of moulding the mind, when it is young, is the correct one and the best approach for forming men and women of character and gentleness, with an ingrained regard for what is right and just.

If this little book can speak for itself—if it interests, educates and moulds at least one young mind into becoming a good, if not great, man or woman and citizen of India—I am satisfied; while to you, the parent who buys it, this gift for your little boy or girl will have been a sound investment.

Kenneth Anderson

# A Word to the Children
# Who Read It

I have written this book especially for you, and I do hope you like the stories it contains. They are a little different from those you may have read up to this time, but I have tried to make them interesting all the same.

These tales are about animals. My reason for relating them is to get you to know more about the animals and birds that live along with us; and if you know a little more about animals you are sure to come to love them and be kind to them. You should remember that the same God that made you and me made these creatures also, and therefore you have no right to be cruel to them in any way.

In each story there is a lesson for you to learn; in some cases, several lessons. The wonderful thing is that these lessons are not taught to us by people but by the humble creatures that many of us think have no feelings or sense of any kind. After reading these tales, I am sure you will agree with me that wild animals and birds, and domestic creatures also, do have sense and feelings after all. And if they can teach us such good and valuable lessons, do you not think we should learn those lessons and follow them, and be kind to the creatures that have taught us?

Should you like these stories and enjoy reading this book, there is a great favour you can do me in return. Will you do it, please? It is quite an easy thing that I ask of you.

Learn the lessons taught here, and make up your mind to be kind to all animals and birds. And tell your friends to be kind too.

When you grow up into men and women, you will be surprised to find that not only did you do me a favour but you have also done something that will reward you very greatly in your everyday life. You will have built up a character for each one of yourselves; and that is something far more precious than money or gold!

Kenneth Anderson

# Bruno, the Sloth Bear

This is the story of a baby sloth bear and all that happened to him for the three years during which he lived.

Before beginning, let me explain briefly that the name 'sloth bear' is given to the only kind of bear that lives in the forests in the centre and south of our country. In the North, there are other kinds of bears too, but the story I am about to relate took place in the South.

Actually, it is quite a wrong name to give this bear, but the reason is because this animal has very long nails on its feet, resembling the long nails growing on the feet of the 'sloth', which is quite a different creature altogether, and lives in a far distant continent called South America. The 'sloth' of South America is to be found on trees, and is something like a monkey. Also, it is very lazy and moves slowly. That is the reason why people who are lazy are often called 'slothful'. The word means that they are full, like a sloth, of laziness.

But the South Indian sloth bear is by no means lazy like the South American sloth. In the wild state in the jungles where it lives, it is true that this bear sleeps nearly all day, but that is because it comes out at night. During that time it is very busy indeed, digging in the earth for roots and the different insects, grubs and white ants, that it feeds upon.

The sloth bear is jet black in colour except for a white mark on its chest. The hair growing on top of its shoulders is extra long, because mother bears, who generally have two babies at a time, carry these babies on their backs when they move about from place to place, and this long hair helps the young bears to have something to hold on to, and to grip, with their sharp little claws and teeth.

The story begins late one evening in a jungle in the south of our country. It was growing dark and a mother bear and her two babies, who had been asleep all day, had just come out of their den in the forest to search for food. The mother bear was walking along a narrow pathway that wound between the bushes, and on her back were perched her two little babies, holding on for all they were worth.

Then a terrible thing happened. Around the corner there stepped a man with a gun in his hand. He was a hunter and quite a cruel man, indeed!

Without thinking or caring, he raised his gun and fired two shots at the poor mother bear who happened to be walking along innocently, only a few feet in front of him.

The first shot struck her right in the middle of her forehead. She fell backwards, and the second shot went through her chest. The mother bear did not move after that, for she was dead.

But the hunter was not as brave as he was cruel. He did not come near the dead bear at once, thinking perhaps she might not be dead at all, but only wounded, and that she would bite or tear him with her claws, if he came too close.

After a while, however, when he saw that the bear did not move, he walked up to the body, where he made a very sad discovery.

His second bullet, in passing through the mother bear's chest, had come out through her back and had killed one of the two baby bears that had been perched there. The other bear cub, which was alive and unhurt, was still clinging on to its mother, not realizing that she was dead.

Even that wicked hunter felt sorry then, for what he had done, and determined that he would take the little bear home and give it to his wife and son. He knew they would look after it and care for it, while if he left it in the jungle, it would surely die of starvation, or be killed by some wild animal, without its mother to feed and protect it.

The baby bear did not want to let go of its parent and made a good deal of noise, but the man caught it by the back of its neck, pulled it of the dead body of its mother, and put it into a large canvas bag that was slung across his shoulder. Then he took the cub home, and gave it to his wife and son.

They were delighted. His wife put a pink ribbon around the cub's neck, kissed him on his little black nose, and called him 'Bruno', for he was a boy cub. The hunter's son also picked him up and played with the little bear, giving him milk to drink and sweets to eat. Bruno did not appear to be at all frightened or shy now. On the other hand, he soon made friends with all the people of the household, and grew to be quite at home.

From that day, the little fellow became almost like a child in that family, and was treated as one. Even the cruel hunter who had shot his poor mother, was more sorry than ever for the deed that he had done, as he, too, grew to love little Bruno more and more each day.

When he first came, Bruno liked to drink milk from a bottle like a baby. But he soon gave up this practice, and would eat and drink anything that was given to him. He did not lap like a dog or cat, but would place his long lips inside the tray or pan, or whatever it was in which the food was served, and draw it up into his mouth and stomach with a loud, sucking sound, as if he had some big pump working inside him.

Another habit to which the young bear was very accustomed, was to suck one of the paws on his legs, and sometimes his own knee, with a loud, humming sound, resembling the noise made by a whole lot of bees when they are swarming.

The hunter and his wife, whom I shall call Mr and Mrs Singh, and their son, Kamal, tried for a long time to discover what was the cause of this habit. But they were not successful. Later they found out that nearly all bears follow this practice. Then they thought that it might just be a bad habit among sloth bears in general.

As a matter of fact, this is not a bad habit among these animals at all. They suck their own paws and knees because they like the taste of the salty sweat that comes out at these places. Bears are very fond of salt, and will eat whole handfuls of it, if you give it to them.

As he grew older and older, Bruno became more and more mischievous. Mr and Mrs Singh had a number of dogs, and Bruno got very friendly with all of them. He would gobble up his own share of food quickly, and then go and rob from the plates in which the dogs were eating. The dogs would growl and try to snap at him, but he would just close his eyes and go on sucking up the dogs' food, till all of it had disappeared in a matter of seconds.

Every morning, Mr Singh would take him out for a walk, along with the dogs. At times, they would meet another lady or gentleman, also out for a walk with their dogs. Before Mr Singh could stop them, Bruno and the dogs would give chase, of course, only in play, and with no intention of harming or biting the other dogs. But the strange lady or gentleman would not know this. It was a funny sight to see them running away for all they were worth, with their pet dog held high in the air to save it from Bruno and the pack of dogs with him.

Although Mr Singh could not help laughing, he often got into trouble over this, as the lady, or gentleman, would go to the police station and make a report. Then a policeman would come along and tell Mr Singh that he should keep Bruno chained, and would threaten to fine him.

Once, when they were all going for a walk, Mr Singh and his pets passed a tennis court where four men were playing tennis. Seeing the ball bouncing about was too much of a temptation for Bruno. Immediately, he ran on to the court, chased and caught the tennis ball, and ran away with it in his mouth. The four men who were playing, were so frightened, that they left the court and ran in all directions. Mr Singh had a hard time getting the ball back out of Bruno's mouth. When he finally succeeded, it was of no use anyhow, for Bruno had bitten it through and through with his strong teeth, and his master had to pay for a new ball.

As he grew bigger, the little bear not only became more mischievous, but more and more greedy, and developed a number of bad habits.

One of these was, that he got to know at what time in the morning the servant woman usually returned from the market, carrying a big basket containing all the provisions she had bought.

So he did a very naughty thing. He hid behind a tree until the woman had come close, and then rushed out at her, holding on to her legs, and trying to reach for the basket on her head. The woman of course, thought he was going to bite her. She screamed with fright, threw the basket down, and ran away, whereupon Bruno ate up every single thing in the basket, leaving just the firewood.

The servant complained, with tears in her eyes, to her master and mistress, but as they had grown very fond of Bruno, they did not like to punish him and excused him, instead. As a result, there was nothing to eat for lunch that day, as Bruno had gobbled it all up. He had made sure of his lunch by eating everyone else's instead!

The following morning, the naughty Bruno did the same thing. He chased the servant as she came from the market, and once more ate up all the contents of her basket. She complained again, and said she would not work there the following day.

This time, Mr Singh had to give Bruno a beating and chain him up. He also had to keep him chained every morning, an hour before the servant woman was due to come from the market.

On another day, Mr Singh had changed the oil in the engine of his car and had kept the old oil, which was black and very dirty, in an empty tin in the garage. Bruno found this and drank it all up. Nearly one gallon of dirty oil! Everyone thought he would get very sick and die. But nothing happened to him at all!

There was a day, however, when Bruno did something very naughty through which he nearly lost his life. It came about in this way.

As you know, rats and mice are very numerous in old houses and do a lot of damage. They had destroyed some papers in Mr Singh's office room, which made him angry, and so he put a lot of rat poison there for them to eat and die, closing the door so that neither Bruno, nor any of the dogs, could enter and eat the poison by accident.

But Bruno was very clever; or rather he thought he was very clever. He climbed in through the window and ate some of this poison.

An hour later he became very very sick. His master knew what had happened. He went in his car and fetched the animal doctor to try to save Bruno's life.

The doctor was a clever man. Bruno was too ill to be able to swallow, but the doctor gave him many injections. With all that, it took nearly two hours before he was able to open his eyes. Do you know he was such a greedy little bear that, an hour later, he wanted to eat again!

Another strange habit this bear formed was to cuddle and fondle a piece of dead tree-root against his breast, as if it was a baby bear of his own. I am sure I could not tell you where he found this tree-root or how he got hold of it, but one day the Singhs noticed he was holding on to something hard, kissing it with his long, thick lips, and licking it with his tongue. When they went closer, they saw it was just a hard bit of dead root. But Bruno would not let go of it. Day by day he would hug and play with his strange toy, till his owners called it his baby.

On another day, Kamal got hold of a piece of bamboo about four feet long, which in play he pointed at Bruno and kept saying, 'I'm going to shoot you! I'm going to shoot you!'

Straightaway Bruno grabbed the other end of the bamboo with his paw, and then very cleverly held it in the crook of his arm and pointed it back at Kamal. Everybody laughed at this, and Kamal left the bamboo with him.

Very often after that, when anybody went near him, Bruno would point the bamboo at them, so that in the end this stick was called 'Bruno's gun'.

Bruno kept these two strange toys of his, his 'baby' and his 'gun', with him till the day he died.

In about two years' time, this bear had grown very big indeed, although he still hugged his 'baby' and pointed his 'gun'. People began to get scared of him, because he had very long teeth and sharp claws on his feet. Mr and Mrs Singh also became afraid that he might bite one of the children belonging to their tenants, or their neighbours, when they called in at the house sometimes. They thought over the matter, and finally decided to send Bruno to a zoo.

The nearest zoo was in a town nearly 90 miles away. Mr Singh wrote to the officer-in-charge, asking if he would like to have Bruno as a gift. The zookeeper replied, accepting the present, and a week later, sent a lorry with a cage in it, in which to fetch Bruno.

The bear cried bitterly, and so did his mistress, when he was forced into the cage, which was then lifted on to the lorry. Mr Singh felt very sad, too, to see him go. He had been such a sweet and affectionate pet. Then the lorry drove away.

But that's not the end of the story.

As I have related, Mrs Singh cried a great deal when Bruno was taken away. A week later, a friend happened to be going to the town where the zoo was to which Bruno had been sent. She asked this friend to visit the zoo to find out how Bruno was getting along.

The friend returned two days later with sad news. Bruno had become very thin, and the zookeeper said he was always crying, particularly at night, and had hardly eaten anything.

Both Mr and Mrs Singh were very upset when they heard this news. Mrs Singh wrote immediately to the officer-in-charge of the zoo, inquiring more about Bruno.

The man wrote back. He said the same thing. The bear was always crying, would hardly eat, although they had offered him all kinds of food, and was becoming very thin indeed. He added that Bruno was no doubt missing his old mistress and master, and could not forget them. It appeared as if he would never settle down in his new home in the zoo and might pine away till he died.

When a pet animal behaves like this, and refuses to eat after he has been separated from his master or mistress, it is called 'fretting'.

After receiving the letter from the zookeeper, Mrs Singh cried bitterly again. She said that she wanted to go and visit Bruno.

At first, her husband did not agree. He knew that such a visit would make her more sad. But Mrs Singh was determined, and said she would go by train if he did not take her by car. So finally he consented, and they both set out by car for the town where the zoo was.

Before they could even reach his cage, the Singhs could hear poor Bruno crying to himself. And when he saw them, what a change took place! He screamed and screamed with joy. So much so, that many people came running to see what it was all about.

Mrs Singh was very happy. She bought him ice cream and buns at the canteen. Bruno ate it all, for he was starving, and wanted more.

All day the Singhs stayed with him. When evening came and the visitors had to leave, poor Bruno cried very bitterly again. As they got into their car on the road far away, the Singhs could still hear him screaming.

So there and then they made up their minds. They would stay the night in some hotel and not go back. The following morning, they would ask the zookeeper to let them have their pet back.

Early next morning, they returned to the zoo. From the road once again, they could hear the bear crying and knew he had been crying all night. But how he shrieked with joy when they stood before his cage once more!

A little later, the officer-in-charge of the zoo arrived, and both Mr and Mrs Singh asked him to please give their pet back to them. He happened to be a kind-hearted man, and agreed readily.

So they fetched a wooden box, put Bruno inside, got men to lift the box on to the top of the car, where they tied it on securely, and were soon on their 90-mile journey back home.

This time, to avoid any danger of Bruno biting the tenants' or neighbours' children, the Singhs thought of a clever plan.

They called labourers to dig a wide and deep trench around a small square-shaped bit of ground, which they left as an island in the centre. Then they built a little brick house on the island for Bruno, and knew if they put him there he would be quite happy, while at the same time the children who came to the house, would be safe from Bruno, as he could not cross over the trench to harm them, nor could they cross over to go near him. The carpenters also built a sort of drawbridge with two old ladders, across which the Singhs and Kamal could go on to the island themselves, to feed the bear and play with him and pet him.

It took nearly ten days for the labourers and carpenters to finish their work, and during this time, Bruno had to remain shut in the box in which he had been brought from the zoo. But never once did he cry, for he knew his old mistress and master were near him all the time.

At last the work was finished. The box was carried across the drawbridge of ladders and Bruno was set free on his island. Mrs Singh gave him back his 'baby' and his 'gun'. Both these things she had kept carefully in memory of Bruno since the day the zoo men had come and taken him away in the lorry.

What a happy day that was for Bruno! How he howled with pleasure and delight, hugged his 'baby', pointed his 'gun', and ate his fill of all the nice things his master and mistress gave him!

The trench was too deep and wide for Bruno or the children to cross, but certainly not too wide for his doggy friends to jump over. All of them visited him several times a day and he was filled with joy once again.

Diwali came shortly after that. As a gift, Mrs Singh gave him a large stuffed teddy bear which she had bought. But this, I am sorry to tell you, Bruno played with so roughly, that he soon tore it to bits. Mr Singh was more wise. He gave him a bag of nuts, which Bruno thoroughly enjoyed.

In this manner another eighteen months passed. Bruno was now a fully grown sloth bear, three and a half years old, very large in size, very fierce to look at, but just as sweet and gentle in nature. Nobody would go on the island except Mr and Mrs Singh and Kamal and their four dogs. All seven knew that Bruno would never bite any of them.

Suddenly Mrs Singh became very ill. She was taken to hospital and Bruno never saw her again. The doctors there did everything they could to cure her, but she got worse and worse, and finally died.

Each morning Bruno would climb on to the roof of his little house in the middle of the island, stand up on his two hind legs, look forth for his mistress and cry bitterly. All day long he would cry, and most of the night, too. But his mistress never came back to him.

After some days, he refused to eat any food. Mr Singh and his son tried to console him, and feed him with bread, milk, cake, nuts and all sorts of nice things. But he met them with tears in his eyes and ate nothing. Day by day he grew more thin. Day after day he cried for the mistress who did not come back.

Exactly three months to the very day after his mistress had died, poor Bruno himself died early in the morning. Mr Singh and his son were with him till the end. There were tears in the big bear's eyes as he breathed his last—tears for the mistress who had left him and had never come back to see him again!

And there were tears in Mr Singh's eyes, and in Kamal's eyes too, as they watched their dear pet die before them, of a broken heart. For yes, his loyal and loving heart was broken indeed.

They buried him along with his 'baby' and his 'gun' that evening. If there is a heaven where people and animals go to when they die, I am sure he must be happy there now, along with his toys, together once again with his beloved mistress.

# The Brave Hyena

A hyena is a curious-looking animal indeed. It is shaped something like a dog but has stripes like a tiger. Even its walk is peculiar. It seems to halt or hesitate every little while, as if in doubt. Perhaps it is in constant fear all the time. Its form is unusual, too. The head and forepart of the body are large and strong, but its back slopes down to hind legs that are much smaller and weaker than the front. The big bushy tail, dark grey in colour, is almost like a brush. All the time that it looks at us, this small animal appears to be crying, for we can see what seem to be tears in its large black eyes. That is why people sometimes call this creature the 'crying hyena'.

This strange beast is found almost all over our country, but mainly in the jungles. Some of the people who also live in the forests all their lives think it is half a tiger and half a dog. Actually it has nothing to do with a tiger at all, but is more of a dog, although there are some important differences.

The hyena hides all day and only comes out at night to search for something to eat. You see, both tigers and panthers don't finish every bit of the animals they kill. There are always some scraps left over, and of course plenty of bones, and these remains are what the hyena lives on for food, together with any other creatures that die in the forest due to other causes. Because of this habit, many people think he is a very filthy animal. Rarely does a hyena succeed in catching anything alive. He moves too slowly to be able to do so, and is rather timid.

Really, a hyena is not a dirty animal at all. As a matter of fact, he is quite clean. Unlike some of our dogs, the hyena keeps his hair and skin free of all dirt by constantly licking himself.

I had one as a pet till quite recently. He was very tame and used to come with me for long walks along the roads and across the countryside. All the people who passed by and saw him were frightened, but he was perfectly harmless and had a most sweet nature. He was particularly fond of dogs and was ready to play with every one of them he met, although some of the dogs were rude in return and wanted to snap and bite at him. No doubt this was because he looked so funny to them.

Now I shall tell you how I came to get this animal, and all that happened in a jungle one night that led me to finding him. This story will show you that, although the hyena looks such an ugly and horrible beast, it is capable of performing a most noble action.

I was once sitting at night on top of a high rock, overlooking the bed of a dry stream. All round me was dense jungle, for I had purposely chosen this quiet spot. When I want to see wild animals, I go to a forest on a moonlit night, sit on a tree or rock, place a few broken branches in front of me so that I will be hidden and not seen, watch animals all night long as they roam about freely in the jungle. Sometimes they come quite close to me, without ever knowing that I am hiding nearby.

Some of the animals you see in a circus and zoo are here in these jungles. To name a few: there are elephants, tigers, panthers, bears, bison—which are really wild cattle—and several kinds of deer. There are also many sorts of smaller creatures which you have perhaps never seen, and whose names you do not know.

## THE BRAVE HYENA

The night my story begins, the rock on which I was sitting, as I have already told you, was by the side of a dry stream-bed. That is, it was dry everywhere else except for a small pool of dirty water that had collected in a hollow right in front of me. It was now in the middle of the hot weather and all the grass and trees were very dry.

Before climbing up the rock, I had noticed the footprints of a number of animals that had visited this pool the previous night, and I hoped I would be able to see them for myself if they came again.

Once the sun sets, it gets very dark in a jungle, and also very frightening. If you are alone, you feel that all sorts of terrible creatures are watching you from under the trees where you cannot see them, getting ready to spring upon you and kill you at any moment. You cannot get over the feeling that hidden eyes are looking at you from dark corners.

So that evening, when the sun went down and it began to grow dark so rapidly, I became afraid too. I wondered if a tiger might come and see me perched on top of the rock. It was not too high for him to spring up at me! I knew it would take another hour for the moon to rise, but before then it would be very dark and if a tiger came, I would not be able to see him.

Now and again I could hear sounds in the jungle, some of them far away and other quite close. A sambar, which is a kind of deer, larger than the spotted deer and fully brown in colour, called in the darkness: 'Dhank! Oonk! Oonk!' It seemed frightened of something, as the sound it was making was a cry of alarm. In the bushes and long grass below the rock, I could hear faint rustling noises as if something was creeping through them and coming closer and closer to where I was sitting. It was far too dark to see anything, and I was becoming more and more frightened. I felt the hair at the back of my neck standing on end.

After a while everything became a little more clear and I knew that something I had been expecting was coming. Then it appeared over the tops of the forest trees to the east. At first it was huge and like a big red ball of fire, but as it climbed higher it seemed to grow smaller and smaller, while changing its colour from red to a shining silver.

In a short half hour the moon had risen! The moonlight I had been waiting for so anxiously, had come at last! It grew almost as bright as day and I could see every bush and blade of grass distinctly, and with its coming, I didn't feel quite so frightened of any beast that might have been hiding below me.

But not for very long!

'O-o-o-ongh! Aungh-ha! Aungh! Ugh! Ugh!'

The sound crashed through the silence, as suddenly, a loud, deep roar came from beneath the trees of the forest on the opposite bank of the dry stream. Then it was repeated three or four times.

It was a tiger!

He was hiding somewhere in front of me! Would he attack? No wonder the sambar had been so terrified a moment ago when he had sounded his alarm cry.

All this while, a number of frogs were croaking on the banks of the muddy pool of water that lay below me: 'Korr! Korr! Korr! Korr!'

The next minute they had all stopped croaking together. Why was this? What was frightening them now? Then I knew the answer.

They had stopped because they had seen the tiger. And I could see him myself, too, as he stepped out from behind the dark shadows under the trees. He was a beautiful animal to look at; huge in size, clearly marked with black stripes across his brown hair that seemed to be grey in appearance!

The tiger walked boldly to the edge of the water, crouched down on the sand, bent his head and began to drink. I could clearly hear the sound of him, lapping up the water.

He drank deeply for about five minutes, stood up, gently shook his head, and then walked forward till he reached the foot of the rock on which I was sitting.

I was trembling all over with excitement and fear, not knowing what was going to happen next. Would the tiger look up and see me hiding on the rock? Would he spring at me then?

But to my good luck he didn't look up. I lost sight of him as he passed close beneath, and then a second later I heard a faint swishing sound as he entered the grass. There was silence after that and I knew the tiger had gone and I was safe.

Not long afterwards there came a loud, twanging sound from the jungle behind me, followed by a great thud. And seconds later

I heard a sharp screeching: 'Tri-a-a-ank! Tri-a-aank!'

The elephants had arrived!

One of them had broken a big branch off a tree and it had fallen to the ground. That was what had caused the twanging twice, to alert the other members. Very likely he saw, or smelt, the tiger that just passed.

The herd came nearer, and at last, with a loud breaking of more branches and tearing of the bushes all around, they marched on to the dry stream-bed, one after the other, about a hundred yards away.

I could count five of them. There was a mother, followed by a very small baby who could just about toddle along behind her. Next came a young elephant that was no taller than I. The fourth was a half-grown male elephant. He had short tusks which I could see quite clearly. The last was a huge, tall animal, about ten feet in height, with long tusks that looked very white in the bright moonlight.

One behind the other, the five elephants walked to the muddy pool and entered it without hesitation. Very soon the water became too deep for the little baby. He started to cry and squeal in alarm, making a funny sound somewhat like a young pig: 'Quink! Quink! Quink!'

But the mother elephant was there to help him. She stretched out her trunk beneath him and lifted him up so as to keep his head above water. The little fellow began to enjoy this. His squeals of fear turned into squeals of delight.

After throwing water over themselves and each other, the five elephants came out of the pool and stood on the dry sand of the stream-bed. Then, what do you think they did next? Why, they started throwing sand over themselves and each other, till they were covered and as dirty as they had been before bathing! Perhaps this was their way of drying themselves, as they had no towels!

It took almost an hour to do all this. Then the five of them marched off into the jungle, one behind the other, in the same order as they had arrived. I could hear them breaking branches and making a noise for sometime afterwards, till finally there was silence.

My watch showed the time to be past 10 p.m.

Suddenly, I was aware of something grey coming down the dry bed of the stream towards the pool. It moved in a funny way. It would come forward a few steps, then stop. Then come forward, and stop again!

When it stood almost opposite me I could make out the grey form and black stripes of a hyena, and could see its black snout and upright ears.

The hyena seemed to be afraid of something behind it. Every little while it would stop, turn its head backwards, and look around. I wondered what it was that could be frightening the beast.

Finally it made up its mind to drink water. It must have been very thirsty, for it darted to the edge of the pool and started lapping very fast, as if to drink as quickly and as much as it could, before running away again.

Only then did I come to discover why the hyena seemed to be so frightened, for behind him I could now observe a number of forms slinking along the banks of the dry stream. They came nearer and nearer, and then suddenly, with shrill calls which you would never for a moment think came from any animal as they, rushed upon the unfortunate hyena together.

In the moonlight I could recognize these creatures now. I counted six of them. They were wild dogs!

Wild dogs in our jungles behave very much like the wolves you must have read about that live in the cold lands of the north. They hunt in packs, as do our jackals, but are much more fierce, and kill and eat other animals, mainly deer and pigs, which they tear to bits and eat almost alive. They are very cruel also, and cunning by nature. They even attack bears, panthers and tigers, and all living creatures, except the elephants, are afraid of them.

While wandering in the jungles, I have several times come across the bodies of tigers that have been torn to shreds and eaten by wild dogs. Of course, the tiger puts up a great fight and kills a great many of his attackers before he himself is killed, but these beasts are so fierce and greedy, and number so many, that they eat not only the tiger after they have killed it, but their own friends that the tiger has killed.

But unlike the scavengers I have told you about, wild dogs do not touch any dead thing they may come across, they must kill it, and then eat.

They were far too fast for him. He had scarcely gone a few yards when they were upon him and a terrible fight commenced.

The hyena was bigger and stronger and could bite harder than any of its attackers, but by nature it is not a fighter, nor can it think and move so quickly. Also it was alone, while the dogs were half a dozen in number.

They jumped on the poor hyena and bit it all over, while it fought back as best as it could.

Luckily, the hyena was able to catch one of the attackers by its throat, and gave it such a great crunch that the wild dog died at once. But the others would not let go and kept on biting the unfortunate hyena. I knew it would soon be killed.

I wanted to save the poor thing, but I had no gun with me and was afraid of getting down from my rock to go near the fighting animals, in case any of them, particularly the wild dogs who were in a great rage and very excited, should turn on me and perhaps kill me too.

So, from the top of the rock I started to

shout, clap my hands, and make as much noise as I could.

For a minute or two, none of the fighting animals heard, as they were intent upon biting one another. Then one of the wild dogs looked up and saw me. He stopped attacking the hyena, and soon the others did so too. Then the five of them stared at me boldly, no doubt very cross because I had interfered at such a time.

The hyena took this opportunity to slink away, but I could see in the moonlight that it had been badly bitten and was covered with blood. One of its hind legs appeared to be dragging along the ground.

It disappeared behind the rock on which I was sitting, while I kept making clicking noises with my thumb and finger to get the wild dogs to keep looking at me to give the hyena a chance of escaping.

For about five minutes they stood and stared. Then they must have realized that I was too high up on the rock and they could not reach me. Also, they were cunning and knew if they followed the hyena they would be able to catch up with it again, and kill and eat it.

So once more, making their hunting call that I have told you sounds like the cries of some strange bird, the remaining five dogs began to run the way the hyena had gone, sniffing the ground and following the trail of blood that had dripped from it.

Nearly ten minutes later, far away in the distance, I could hear the sounds of fighting once again, and knew that the hyena was being killed.

No animals came to the pool to drink water for the rest of that night, although I kept awake till morning. I suppose the noise of the fight that had taken place must have been heard all over the jungle and frightened everything away.

Next morning, when the sun rose and it became a bit warm, I climbed down from the rock and followed that trail of blood that had been left behind by the hyena in its flight. I wanted to find out how the matter had ended.

There was a small hill by the side of the dry stream, and it was from here that I had heard the sounds of the fight being continued after the dogs had caught up with the hyena. Quite a lot of blood had dripped on to the ground from the wounded beast, so there was no difficulty in locating the place where the battle had finally ended.

I came upon the dead body of the hyena at last, or rather I should say, some torn bits of striped skin and a few bones. All the rest had been eaten by the dogs.

The poor animal must have fought well, for I also saw the remains of a second dog that had been killed by it. This dog had also been eaten by its companions before they had gorged themselves sufficiently to leave the spot.

**40**

After looking sadly at all that remained of the gallant hyena, I turned to walk away, when I heard a faint sound. It was something like the sound you must have heard young kittens making; a sort of faint mewing.

I looked around at once to see where it was coming from.

A few yards away were five or six large rocks heaped together one upon the other, and below them was a space leading underground. Standing just outside this hole, or low cave, was a baby hyena. He was looking very sorrowfully at me, and at the remains of the big hyena that had been killed. Even from that distance I could see what looked like tears glistening in the corners of his large eyes. I knew that he was weeping for his mother.

Only then did I realize that the brave mother could have prolonged her life by running into the cave where she lived with her baby, but hadn't done so for fear that the cruel wild dogs would follow her into the hole and eat up her puppy. So she had decided to remain outside and fight them, although she knew that in doing so she would surely be killed. But at least the dogs would go away after that with their bellies full, and would not think of searching inside the cave. What a heroic action, indeed!

I caught that baby hyena and brought it back home. He was a male and I called him 'Jackie'. I kept him as a pet till he was four years old. Lots of children, and big people too, even visitors from England, America and Germany, came to my house to see him, and they were all very thrilled to see how tame he was.

# The Wise Old Elephant

This is the story of a wise old elephant who once lived in one of the great forests of our country.

Lots and lots of other animals lived with him in that jungle. There were tigers and panthers, deers and crocodiles, birds and snakes, and all kinds of wonderful creatures. But of all of these, this old elephant became the king, and I will tell you how and why he became king.

As you know, it does not rain throughout the year in our country. In fact, for eight or nine months it does not rain at all, and the land becomes hot and dry and parched. Then, in the middle of the year, after the hottest season, down comes the rain; and when it does come, it rains hard for days and days and days. It is almost as if the rain is trying to make up for not coming all the rest of the year.

In the forests, the pools and the rivers store up this rainwater and keep it for many months, and it is from these pools and rivers that the birds and the animals, and all the other creatures of the jungle, have to drink water to keep themselves alive during the dry period.

Year after year, by the end of the hot weather, but before the rain starts, there is very little water left anywhere. The leaves fall from the trees, the grass withers and dries, and the animals become thin and starved. The koel, a bird that you may have often heard in your garden, cries out for rain. In the hot afternoons, when the sun is beating down without mercy and the animals and other creatures look anxiously at the clear sky, longing for the clouds to appear which will bring the rain, this bird can be heard calling to the gods to send the rain quickly: 'Ko-el! Ko-el! Ko-el!' And what is most wonderful to relate, the gods generally hear this bird and send the rain within a few days to water the forests.

But one year, long ago, the gods became angry with the villagers and determined to punish them by sending no rain that year. And because of the sins of these wicked men, the poor koel and the other birds and wild animals in the forest, who were innocent themselves, had to suffer. The koel cried aloud for water, but her call was in vain. The rain never fell. The animals in the jungle panted with thirst, but still there was no rain. At last, a time came when they made up their minds that they would all have to die.

So they arranged a meeting in order to decide what they should do.

But before such a meeting could be held, the animals had to first come to an agreement among themselves. The tigers had to promise not to kill the deers that came to the meeting, and the panthers had to promise not to harm any other creatures either.

The monkeys served as messengers to carry the invitation to each of the animals in turn to attend this meeting. They knew they were safe in talking to the tigers while giving this message, for they could hang by their tails and legs high up in the trees, out of reach.

When the tigers and panthers heard about the meeting they were glad, for they were thirsty too and very frightened as well, but were not clever enough to be able to think what should be done and wanted the help of the other animals, who were more clever, in showing them a way to get the water they needed so much.

At last all the beasts met together under the shade of a very large banyan tree that was growing in the heart of the forest.

The monkeys, who had arranged the meeting, took the lead. They told the animals who had gathered there that something had to be done soon to get water, or all of them would die of thirst.

A sly old jackal then had an idea.

'That's easy,' he said, 'all you monkeys have to do is to climb to the tops of the coconut palms in the forest, break off the nuts that are growing there, and are full of water, and throw them down to us.'

The animals were happy at hearing these words. They said the jackal was a very clever fellow to have thought of such an idea and all of them set off behind him to the nearest grove of coconut trees in the jungle to get the coconut water.

The monkeys scampered up the tall coconut palms and soon bit off the nuts from the tops of the trees. They began to throw them to the ground, and the animals ran to pick them up and drink the water that they thought was inside.

But, alas, they were greatly disappointed. For in falling from the tall palm trees, the nuts hit the ground so hard that most of them burst and the coconut water spilled into the parched earth before the animals had any chance to drink it.

The poor creatures huddled together at the foot of the coconut trees after that. They were desperate and filled with fear. For they were very thirsty and the only plan they had thought of had failed.

Just then an old elephant among them had another idea. Up to this time, none of the other animals had even troubled to ask this elephant's advice, for to them he looked rather a stupid fellow. Although he was very large in size, he had a mild temper and did not harm any of the other creatures. In fact, they were less afraid of him than they were of the tigers, the panthers, the wolves and the wild dogs that lived in the jungles. All of these killed any animal they could catch, and sometimes each other, but the big old elephant did not harm even a little bird or a mouse.

'I am growing old now,' he began, 'but I remember that, over fifty years ago, before any of you were born, the rains had failed to come, just as they have failed this year, and everything dried up.

'I was searching for water one day when I came to the bed of a stream. There was no water in it and the stream was quite dry.

'But for some reason that I don't know, I began to scrape with my front feet and dig with my trunk in the sand. Perhaps it was just idleness that made me dig. Maybe, I was angry.

'Anyway, I dug, and I dug, and I dug.

'Then I noticed a strange thing. As I went deeper the sand began getting cooler and cooler.

And it was not so dry. In fact, it was becoming moist.

'The thought came to me that I might find water in this way. So I began to dig harder, faster and deeper.

'I dug quite a deep hole and a large one, and right enough, I found water! I drank, and drank, and drank.

'They all came and drank, and they were very happy after that and thanked me very much, too.

'But I must tell you that all this happened in another jungle, quite far from here,' concluded the old elephant. 'I know there is a stream in this forest, and that it is dry now. But I don't know if I will be able to find any water should I dig in it, like I did that day, many years ago.'

There followed a chorus of pleadings from all the other animals that heard him. Even the tigers, and the big bison and wild buffaloes that had come to the meeting, began to beg of him. 'Please, please try,' they asked, 'for we are so very, very thirsty.'

The obliging old elephant immediately agreed to try, and they all trooped off behind him to the dry bed of the stream, just a mile away.

The elephant selected a spot where the sand seemed soft, and there he began to dig with one of his large, powerful front legs and with his long trunk.

It was hard work, at first, for him to shift away the loose sand. But seeing what was required, the sloth bear and the porcupine started to help him. Soon the mongoose and the pangolin, which is a small animal that has scales on it like armour, began to dig too. Then the wild pigs joined in.

They dug and they dug, while the elephant cleared away the loose earth as fast as he could with his trunk and feet.

They worked hard and for a long time.

Then they noticed the sand becoming wet

and more loose and more soft. So they dug even harder and faster and deeper.

At last the sand became quite dark in colour, for it was damp, and they could get the smell of water. They dug even harder after that.

Finally they came upon a tiny trickle of muddy water that showed through the sand, and they dug yet harder and faster still.

In about four hours, the animals had made a large hole in the bed of the stream which soon filled with the life-giving water that had been running underground all this time, but was too little to show itself at the surface, and which they had known nothing about.

The animals drank their fill after that. But the big old elephant, although he was very thirsty and had worked so hard, and although it had been his idea to dig and find the water, waited till all of them had finished before he began to drink. Remember, he was a huge animal, bigger than any of them, and could have easily pushed them aside had he wanted.

When he had finished drinking, the elephant looked up and found all the animals still gathered around him. He was surprised that they had not gone away and wondered what they wanted.

So he asked them, 'Do any of you want more water?'

'We are waiting to thank you,' they answered in a chorus, 'and to make you our king. For you are the wisest of us all, the strongest and yet the most generous and gentle.'

Then, by common consent, one by one, all those animals, large and small, filed past the old elephant to thank him for saving their lives. Many of them had tears of gratitude in their eyes. Even the tiger, who had been considered by most of them to hold this title, was glad to give it up now.

And that was how the wise old elephant became the King of the Jungle, a distinction that is held by him and his descendants to this day.

The truce between the animals continued for a long time. They all drank from that water-hole in the stream-bed, nor did one harm the other for many weeks, till at last the gods forgave the wicked villagers and sent rain.

After that, the stream began to flow and there was plenty of water for everyone in the forest. Then the tigers and panthers, who were in the habit of hunting for their food, told the elephant, their king, and the monkeys, to tell the other animals of the jungle that their truce must now come to an end. They were very hungry, and from the following day would have to once again start killing and eating such creatures as they could catch.

In a later story I will tell you what happened to this same wise old elephant.

# The Lone Jackal

In the jungles and wastelands of our country, are many kinds of animals that belong to the dog family. In a few places there are wolves which look very much like the wolves of northern Europe and America, and resemble Alsation dogs. Then there are hyenas and wild dogs, jackals and foxes.

The most cunning and clever of the lot are the jackals. This story not only shows how artful one of them was, but proves that a clever brain always gets the better of someone or something that is not so intelligent, or that relies mostly on its own strength, rather than its cunning or ability.

Jackals live in families, or 'packs' as they are called, both in jungles as well as round about our villages. Like hyenas and vultures, they are 'scavengers'. This means they eat any dead creature that they may come across, and other stinking things that would remain on the land and smell for days if not taken away.

The thought that dead creatures do lie about in the jungles may surprise you, but it is so, as tigers and panthers will not eat anything that is dead. It is left to the jackals, hyenas and vultures to do so, as well as eat whatever is left of those animals that the tigers and panthers have killed and eaten most of themselves.

The jackal is a handsome animal, the size of an average dog, but grey-brown in colour with a dark bushy tail. It has very pretty grayish-green eyes and pointed ears. Hyenas and vultures, on the other hand, are ugly to look at. But all three of these creatures do a very useful service.

Packs of jackals hide in the jungle all day, or under bushes, or in holes in the ground, and only come out at night in search of food. Sometimes they are very noisy, particularly on moonlit nights, and their cries are so strange and loud that they frighten children who are not accustomed to the sound.

Every pack has a leader, and it is he who starts to call first. He begins with something like this: 'Oo-ooo-ooo! Wooo-ooo-ooo!' Then quickly he changes to: 'Oo-ooo-where! Ooo-where! Ooo-where!' and stops. Now all the jackals in the pack begin to answer him. Very quickly and very loudly, they keep howling: 'Here! Here! Heeere! Hee-eere! Hee-yah! Hee-yah! Yah! Yah!

Now the leader starts again, and keeps up his part of the call, which is: 'Oo-ooo-ooo!

Oo-ooo-where! Oo-ooo-where!' over and over again, while the other jackals keep answering: 'Here! Here! Hee-eere! Heeyah! Yah! Yah!'

These packs of jackals keep searching all night for food, although they do not call all the time. Sometimes they become greedy and come into villages, where they will make off with fowls, or even young goats. On the fields they will eat such small things as lizards, rats, mice and birds that are sleeping on the ground.

As I have said, all jackals are cunning, but at times one of them living in the jungle becomes more cunning than ever. We may even say he becomes wise, for what do you think he does?

Why, a most unusual thing! You may think it is a very dangerous thing to do too, and I agree. But the jackal is so clever that he manages to get away with it safely enough.

He starts following a particular tiger or panther about, everywhere that the animal goes.

The jackal knows that the tiger, or panther, has to kill and eat some animal every two or three days to keep himself alive, so that by following and waiting till his master has finished eating and goes to some river or pool to drink water, the jackal has a chance to grab something that is left of the dead animal for himself, before the tiger can get back. In this way, the jackal is certain of getting regular meals practically every second day without too much trouble to himself.

Of course, the tiger would kill the jackal if he could catch him at any time, particularly when he is robbing; but the jackal is too clever to get caught. While he is gobbling what he has stolen, he keeps a sharp look out with his eyes, ears and nose for the tiger's return. No sooner does he see, hear, or scent his master coming back than he scampers away, safe and out of sight.

Often the tiger gets so accustomed to seeing the jackal following him that he does not try to catch or kill him. So long as the jackal doesn't come too near and within reach of his paws, the tiger begins to take him for granted, and leaves the jackal alone.

When this happens, the cunning jackal is clever enough to know it and at once takes full advantage of the situation. He makes himself almost a partner of the tiger. When he sees some animal which perhaps the tiger has not seen or heard, he calls aloud to attract the tiger's attention. The animal he has spotted does not get afraid, because it thinks the sound comes only from a jackal.

In time, the tiger gets to learn the jackal is calling him to a feast. He attacks and kills the animal that the jackal had first seen, and eats as much of it as he can. Then the jackal eats what is left.

In this way, the mighty tiger and the cunning jackal become almost friends, while the jackal is sure of never going hungry. For is not the tiger there to provide food for him?

Very clever on the part of the jackal, don't you agree?

A jackal that forms the habit of following a tiger, or panther, does not stay with the rest of the pack. For a tiger may tolerate the presence of one jackal. He would certainly not like a number of them following him about. To say the least of it, they would give away his presence to all the creatures of the jungle. Thus the jackal that follows a tiger does so alone and is therefore known as 'the lone jackal'.

When this lone jackal calls to let his partner, the tiger or panther, know he has seen some animal that may be feasted upon, he does not make the same sounds that I have told you about earlier, as made by the leader and the rest of the jackal pack. He utters quite a different call.

It is rather difficult for me to imitate this noise in writing, but I should say it closely resembles the sound that will come if you call the word 'Ba-ooh-ah! Ba-ooh-ah!' three or four times in a loud voice. It is the signal which the tiger has learnt and indicates that the lone jackal has seen something they both can eat, and he hurries to answer the cry.

The story I am now about to relate concerns one such lone jackal, and how he used his cunning brain to escape from certain death.

It was evening, and a tiger had gone down to a pool of water among the rocks a short distance away, to drink and rest awhile.

The lone jackal, which had formed the habit of following this tiger about, was rolling on his back in the sand on the bed of the dry stream that led to the pool where the tiger had gone. The sand was warm, as the sun had been shining on it all day, and the jackal was enjoying this warmth.

Suddenly the lone jackal stopped rolling about and scrambled quickly to his feet. He thought he had heard a sound coming from the long grass and thick bushes that grew along both banks of the dry stream. It had been a faint rustling noise, but the jackal knew that rustling sounds of any kind mean danger. His partner, the tiger, might have become angry for some reason and might even now be creeping upon him. Or it could have been made by a panther, a wild dog, or even a poisonous snake in the grass, all of which creatures were his enemies.

So the lone jackal stood alert, his ears upright and twitching, trying to catch the sound again, while the tip of his nose quivered as he attempted to get the scent of an enemy.

At that moment the wind blew a little towards him, but it was enough. The lone jackal caught the smell at once. It came from his old and most dreaded foe—the panther!

The jackal stared towards a clump of thick bushes and grass that grew on the left bank of the dry stream. Although he could not see anything, he knew for certain that the panther was hiding behind that bush.

He started to think fast. The jackal knew

that within another minute the panther would spring upon him. If he tried to creep away, it would see him and attack sooner. What was he to do at this time of great danger?

Suddenly, the lone jackal remembered his companion. He had been watching the tiger only a few minutes earlier, and knew that it had gone down to the pool of water close by, to drink there. He also knew that tigers do not like panthers, and often kill and eat them. Could he rely upon the tiger to help him now? At any moment that panther would leap upon him, and there could be no escape. The jackal thought and thought fast.

Then, keeping an eye watchfully upon the dense clump of grass and bushes where his enemy lay in hiding, he raised his head to call loudly: 'Ba-oooh-ah! Ba-oooh-ah! Ba-oooh-ah!'

The next moment he started to run as fast as he could down the dry stream-bed towards the pool of water where the tiger had gone.

The panther, who did not suspect his presence had been discovered by the cunning jackal, was just about to spring upon his victim, when he saw the jackal raise his head and call three times in a strange way, 'Ba-ooh-ah!' He had begun to wonder at the unusual sound, when the jackal dashed off at top speed down the stream-bed, and without waiting a moment longer, the panther sprang after him in long, fast bounds.

Jackals can run fast, and this one certainly did his best, but they cannot move as fast as a charging panther, who comes onward in great rapid leaps, roaring as he comes, 'Woof! Woof! Woof!'

The jackal heard the sounds behind him growing ever louder and closer, and he made up his mind that he would be killed. In sheer terror he attempted to run faster still.

'Aar-rumf! Aar-rumf!' Without warning the earth seemed to tremble as those terrible roars came suddenly from in front.

The next instant, a huge shape sprang over him, a mighty reddish-brown and white form, striped with black, directly at the panther who was now very close behind.

It was his partner, the tiger, and he had come to the rescue!

In yet greater terror the jackal ran on and on, while the sounds of a great fight broke out behind, as the panther battled for its life against its mighty cousin, the tiger. But all to no avail.

The tiger had finished drinking water and was lying under a tree, feeling very hungry indeed. Three days had passed since he had eaten. He heard the jackal's urgent call to a feast and bounded up the dry stream in response.

Then he heard another sound that made him very angry indeed. It was the roar made by the panther as he was chasing the jackal.

This infuriated him even more, as he hated panthers anyhow. He concluded that this one must be trying to rob the feast to which the jackal was calling him, and the tiger made up his mind to put an end to his enemy if he could catch him.

So it was that the tiger and panther fought to the death, but it was a battle that did not last very long. With a tremendous blow of his paw, the tiger struck his opponent across its head, and before the smaller animal could recover, bit deeply into its throat. A few minutes later the panther was dead.

Far off, as the noise of growling and snarling came to a stop, the jackal ceased running too. He knew that his companion, the tiger, had won the fight, and that the horrible panther, his enemy, had been killed. He was safe.

So you see that even among the most fierce animals there is a sense of loyalty and friendship.

Had the jackal lost his head, and not called to the tiger, he would surely have been killed, but by using his brains, the jackal was able to outwit an enemy many times larger, stronger and more fierce than himself.

# The Love of an Elephant for His Son

This is the story of how the wise old elephant was brought from the forest, where he lived, to a zoo in one of our cities.

In the jungle this elephant went by the name of 'Yanai'. A word that struck fear into the hearts of all the villagers.

When he was young, Yanai was not a tame elephant as he is now. Children could not go for a ride on his back. On the other hand, he was a very fierce animal and people kept as far away from him as possible. If they saw him in the jungle, or even heard him breaking down the branches of trees, the villagers ran away as fast as they could. This was because other wild elephants, like Yanai, had been known to kill people they met in the forest by chasing and catching them, and then trampling upon them with their huge feet, or beating them against the ground with their trunks.

Do not think for moment, that just because an elephant is such a large animal he cannot move fast. When he wants to do so, an elephant can run nearly as fast as a man, and for a much longer distance too. Also, it is rather easy for him to catch a person in a forest. For a man cannot run through bushes. For one thing the thorns stop him and he has to go around. But when an elephant chases anybody, it just crashes its way through everything, and so can very quickly catch up with the man who is trying to run away from it.

**70**

Well, Yanai lived with his wife and two children in a very beautiful part of the forest for many years, till he became quite an old animal. A lovely stream ran through the jungle that supplied them with water to drink and bathe in during the rainy season. Then in the valleys between the hills, grew many clumps of bamboo. Yanai and his family used to break down these bamboos in order to feed on the young, tender leaves that grew at the very top. The baby elephants were particularly fond of these shoots. On the hillsides there were tamarind trees. When the tamarind pods became ripe, Yanai and his little family, and lots of other elephants too, used to spend whole days and nights beneath these trees, reaching up with their long trunks to break down the ripe pods and stuff themselves till they were full.

Yanai had a lovely pair of tusks, but his wife's tusks were hardly over six inches in length. This is because female elephants do not grow long tusks.

Yanai had two children. Both of them were boys. The first was about ten years old, but still too young for his tusks to show. His name was Hathi. The second was a baby. He had been born hardly a month earlier.

When Hathi saw his baby brother the day he was born, he got quite a shock. For the baby elephant looked almost pink, and was covered with hair. He wondered what this strange thing could be, till his father and mother told him it was his baby brother, and that his name was Kootee.

Within a month, Kootee began to show that he was quite a mischievous baby indeed. When Hathi was not looking, he would sneak forward from under his mother and pull his older brother's tail. Then he would run back there for shelter, when he found Hathi becoming angry at having his tail pulled.

Kootee was still too young to eat any of the bamboo and other leaves on which the elephants fed, or for that matter, the wild fruit either. He drank milk from his mother and spent all his spare time worrying Hathi. But with all that, Hathi was very fond of him, while his mother and Yanai doted on the little fellow and guarded him against the ever-hungry tigers that would have killed and eaten him if they could, as he was not yet three feet high.

Kootee even teased his father, the mighty Yanai, by running about under him and playing. Yanai's tail was too high up for Kootee to reach, so the little fellow made up for it by trying to pull his father's trunk that hung almost to the ground. It was funny to see him teasing his parent, who was such a huge creature. But the old elephant never got angry. He loved his little son very much and was always tender and kind.

About this time a letter was sent from the zoo in Calcutta to the government officer in charge of the forests, who is known as the Chief Conservator, asking for an elephant to be caught and supplied to the zoo. It was to be tamed first before being sent to Calcutta, where it would be used for giving rides to children upon its back.

The Chief Conservator agreed, and ordered the Forest Ranger to set traps in the jungle to catch an elephant. The Forest Ranger serves under the Chief Conservator and is in charge of a particular part of the jungle. He is put there by the government, along with a number of assistants, to look after the forest and see that nobody cuts down the trees or kills the wild animals. There are several of these rangers in every jungle.

So the ranger who had been ordered to trap the elephant, and whose name was Ram, set about his work. He told his assistants to ask the jungle-men, known as Karumbas in this part of the country, to find places where elephants roam regularly, so that he could set his traps there. These Karumbas, having been born in the jungle and having lived all their lives there, know about the habits of the wild animals.

Off they went early one morning to search for tracks and suitable places where there was a chance of catching an elephant, and by evening returned with the good news that they had come across three different pathways followed by the herds of elephants, leading to the little stream in the jungle, where the huge beasts used to drink water twice a day.

When he heard this, Ram gathered all his assistants, and as many Karumbas as he could get, and took them to the first of these pathways. Right in the middle of it he got the men to dig a large pit. It was 12-feet deep by 20-feet long, and was as wide as the pathway itself, which was about ten feet wide.

It took the men many days to dig the pit. This was because they had to carry the earth they had dug in baskets and throw it some distance away, in order to follow the rest of the cunning plan that Ram had made. The work had to be done carefully and as quietly as possible, so as not to make the elephants suspicious of a trap being set.

At last the big pit was finished and every scrap of loose earth had been cleared away.

Ram then made his men gather fallen and rotting leaves and throw them into the pit up to a depth of about three feet. After that they cut bamboos, split them, and made a sort of rough top to cover the pit entirely, from end to end. Over this cover Ram and his men scattered some earth very cleverly, and then planted grass and even small shrubs in that earth, till the bamboos could no longer be seen. In fact, so skilfully did they work, that by the time they were finished, all signs of the pit that had been dug across the pathway, were completely hidden. The path looked just the same as it had before.

Finally, to attract the elephants, Ram told his assistants to gather two baskets of tamarind pods and place them in a big pile right in the centre of his trap. He knew the elephants would pass that way, see the pile of tamarind, and walk forward to eat it, while the thin bamboo cover would not be able to support the great weight of an elephant, and would collapse just as soon as the first of these animals trod upon it, and the elephant would fall into the pit.

Ram had placed dry and rotting leaves at the bottom of the pit. These dry leaves were to form a sort of cushion to break the fall of the elephant, so that it would not hurt itself. Otherwise, being the heavy animal that it was, a fall of about twelve feet into the pit, might have caused the elephant to break a leg.

At last, everything was ready. With a final look around to see that no mistakes had been made, Ram and his followers went back to their quarters to wait patiently, till the Karumbas reported that an elephant had been caught.

They did not have to wait long.

Just two nights later, Yanai and his family walked down that tract.

As is usually the practice with wild elephants when they roam in the jungles, Yanai's wife was leading; Kootee was immediately behind her; then came Hathi; and lastly Yanai, the mighty elephant, their lord and protector. In a family party, the bull elephant, who is the leader, always guards the rear against attack, for it is from behind that the cruel tiger suddenly makes his unexpected leap to kill a helpless baby elephant should its parents be walking in front.

So it was that the mother elephant turned the corner and came upon the trap so cunningly laid by Ram and his men, with the tamarind pods to tempt them.

Something seemed to warn her of danger and she stopped so suddenly that little Kootee bumped his forehead against her hind legs. Suspiciously, the mother elephant looked in front of her, but everything seemed all right at first. The heap of ripe tamarind pods certainly looked very tempting. She thought they looked almost too nice. She wondered how they had got here when there was no tamarind tree anywhere close by.

And then, before she could stop him, Kootee darted between her legs and forwards towards the tamarind. Although he was yet too young to eat it, Kootee was a bit greedy, and that was the cause of the punishment that soon befell him.

Small as he was, he weighed almost three hundred pounds, and that was far too great a weight to be borne by the thin frame of bamboo matting beneath.

There came a crashing sound all at once, and Kootee disappeared from view as he fell into the pit below.

For a moment his mother was so surprised that she did not realize what happened to Kootee. Then she looked down into the pit through the hole in the cover through which he had fallen, and saw Kootee inside. He was squealing with fright and looking up at her very pitifully, and there were large tears streaming from his eyes already.

Kootee's mother became frantic. She trumpeted with rage and fear, not knowing what to do.

Hathi ran behind a tree and hid himself when he heard his mother's screams, while Yanai, thinking some tiger had attacked his wife and little son, rushed forward from the rear to defend them. Indeed, he all but fell into the pit in his haste, and was just saved in time by his wife, who put out her trunk to stop him.

When the old elephant saw what had happened to his baby, he too went mad with rage. His shrieks, added to the screams of his wife, and the squeals of little Kootee from inside the pit, fairly shook the jungle with sound.

Far away in their quarters, Ram and his assistants were disturbed from their sleep by the noise the elephants created and were very pleased. They knew they were lucky and that an elephant must have been trapped.

Meanwhile, both father and mother elephant became yet more desperate in their efforts to rescue their baby. Yanai went down on his knees, and with his mighty tusks, trunk and forelegs, tried to break down the top of the pit. For a short while he succeeded. Then the slope he had dug became too steep and he nearly fell in, head over heels, for the second time.

On her part, Yanai's wife tore down some long bamboos and threw them inside, with their ends resting against the top of the pit. She hoped Kootee would be able to pull himself out by grasping one of the ends with his trunk, while she hauled him out by the other end. But he was too much of a baby to be able to understand her plan.

All night long the parents tried to rescue their little son, but failed. With all that, they kept trying and trying, till the sky in the east began to grow bright and they knew that soon it would be morning.

Old Yanai knelt down once again at the edge of the pit and stretched his trunk inside to the fullest extent until Kootee could just touch it with the tip of his own trunk. But the distance between was a little too far, and there was no grip, while Kootee was still too small and weak to be able to hold on while his father pulled him out of the pit.

The sun was rising above the hills in the east when Yanai thought of a last, desperate plan to save his baby son. He did not tell his wife what he had in mind, for it would only distress her and she would cry and tell him not to do it. Instead, he turned around and stood still to look at his beautiful home, the jungle, for the last time in freedom.

The next moment, old Yanai deliberately jumped into the pit himself!

Once inside, it was easy for him to wind his trunk around little Kootee and lift him high above his head so that the mother elephant could, in turn, also catch him and take him completely out of the pit. At last their precious baby was free. But at what a price!

'What about you?' Yanai's wife asked, fear in her voice and tears in her eyes.

'Alas, I can't get out,' replied Yanai sadly, 'but as long as our son is safe, I'm glad to have been able to set him free.'

Just then they heard the voices of men approaching. In her grief Yanai's wife thought of rushing upon them and killing them, but old Yanai gave her sound advice.

'They will be armed with guns,' he said, 'and will shoot you, Hathi, and Kootee too. Flee while there's yet time to do so. Only think of me sometimes, and when he grows into a big boy, tell Kootee what his father did for him.'

Crying pitifully, Yanai's wife led their sons away, and a few minutes later Ram, the Forest

Ranger, followed by a number of men, came to the spot.

When they saw the huge elephant they had caught, they were very pleased indeed, for they knew they would get a reward from the government when he was sold.

For fifteen days they starved poor Yanai till he became so weak he could hardly stand. Then, when they saw he was in no condition to fight back, with the help of four tame elephants and ropes, they pulled him out of the pit, but not before they had put great iron rings and heavy chains around his feet to prevent him from attacking them or escaping.

They kept him tied in this manner for several months, giving him just enough food to keep him from starving to death.

It was a long time before Yanai became tame enough to be allowed to move about freely, although the heavy iron rings and chains were still kept on his legs.

At last, he was sold by the government for

six thousand rupees, while Ram and the men who had helped him, got a reward of three hundred rupees.

Yanai was put into a special wagon and taken by train to Calcutta where he was lodged in the zoo and taught, little by little, to allow people to ride on his back.

He has been there many years now and has become very friendly with people and especially with little children. He loves to take them for rides on his great broad back.

When he sees children a sad look comes into his eyes. Perhaps his mind and his spirit wander away many thousands of miles at that moment, back to his distant family and his beloved jungles. Maybe he sees his wife and Hathi, and Kootee, who has now become a full-grown elephant himself, safe and happy there. Old Yanai sighs a little then, but he is glad he sacrificed himself so that his family could be free.

And in that distant forest, Yanai's wife still

thinks of her brave husband. She has never ceased to remember him. While Hathi and Kootee try their best to be as big, strong and large-hearted as their father. For elephants never forget!